To Angie

Searching for

by ellora muna

Elena
grandma's friend
and
coworker

ellora muna

Searching for Riki by Ellora Muna

Illustrated by: Gynux

Except Emperor with crown illustration by Ellora Muna

This book is dedicated to a firefly named Suparna

for the light you bring into the world

and to a warrior named Daniel,

for training me to be

a hero.

To my chocolate smelling rose,
far, far away.
You never existed,
yet forever perfumed my life...

-Ellora Muna

CONTENTS

DRAGON

Once upon a time, in a faraway land high up in the Himalayas, there lived a mysterious dragon. Legends told the story of a dragon, who would sweep down and carry the souls of evil men whose hearts had grown cold, selfish and unkind. The dragon would come down and snatch the souls of the selfish, and they could be seen like mysterious lights that would appear and disappear the entire accent of the mountain, never to be heard from again.

Although people searched for the dragon, he remained unseen… yet a legend grew across the land, that no man could see him alive and live.

....

One winter night, a cold breeze carried over an unfamiliar voice; it penetrated all the elements in the universe. Through harsh wind and snow the voice entered the mountain and lit a fire in the dragon's heart.

Unable to hold back his curiosity, the dragon searched the night for the voice and found that standing at the bottom of the mountain was a little girl. She wore a bright yellow shirt tucked in baggy trousers, gathered in tightly at the ankle.

She spoke to the mountain in the language of her heart.

The dragon closed his eyes and listened.

"When will you come back for me?" she asked, as if she knew the dragon was listening. Leaving the mountain, the little girl disappeared into the dark.

The dragon thought of the little girl's question, then retreated into the silent darkness, his heart ablaze.

...

The following evening, the dragon came from within the depths of the mountain hoping the little girl would return. The little girl did return. She stood at the bottom of the mountain and began to speak of her needs. As she spoke, the dragon listened as he had never listened before.

This became a routine; the little girl and dragon would appear and disappear, each seeking the others company at a certain time in their lives, whether knowing or unknowingly.

The dragon fell deeply in love with the little girl's messages to the mountain.

....

There came a day when the dragon could no longer hold back his feelings. When the little girl appeared, the dragon rushed down the mountain to meet her.

He approached her carefully. He stood in front of her, showing the magnificent colors of his wings. Closing his unearthly eyes, he took in her soul, her spirit and the kindness in her being.

"What a beautiful bird you are!" she exclaimed in awe.

The dragon stood still, charmed by her innocence, for it had never been close to a little girl before and she disarmed the feelings in his heart.

Dragon and girl stood in the snow and neither perceived the cold.

"You are stronger than all the elements in the world," the dragon said to her and never said a word aft er that, feeling he had said too much already. He stood magnificent and still.

"Who are you?" asked the little girl, *"You are enchanting to look at."*

The dragon gazed deeply into her eyes for a while.

"I am Tea," she said, ignoring his silence, *"I am named after all the tea gardens here in the Himalayas."*

And the little girl, dressed in pink, spun around like a top in self-defense, for she too was afraid of the feelings in her heart.

The dragon remarked that Tea had the spirit of a mountain flower, one that would bloom under the harshest conditions, because that was its destiny.

Tea had encountered a magical being out in the snow. She looked into the dragon's eyes and saw that it too was vulnerable.

She decided to make her intentions clear.

"Don't leave me," she said.

The dragon, who took the souls of corrupted men, considered the possibility of leaving everything he knew for Tea, but the increased human contact would endanger him.

She would take him home and he would take the soul of someone close to her, for the dragon fed on corrupted hearts.

The proposition was too dangerous. In an extraordinary unfolding of events, the dragon looked at her and said, *"I will come back for you..."*

With no warning, the mighty dragon pushed off its powerful legs and flew away, as if flying out of an open cage — an open universe. He flew so high and so fast that at one point he transformed himself into a dot in the sky... no longer visible to the human eye. Seeing Tea cry was the most painful feeling in the dragon's heart. Yet, his wings took flight and he flew away, never stopping, captivated by the nature of the one he loved.

Dismayed, Tea went home and pulled up a chair and looked into her father's long gold telescope - an instrument he often used to view very large objects that had become very small. Unable to cope with the harshness of the physical world, and the bucket of the dreams in her heart, the little girl longed for the dragon.

STARS

Every day, Tea peeked inside the telescope and searched for the dragon. Where was this unknown place this mystical creature had travelled to?

In her pauses, she thought of him often. And as we frequently do, fondly when we love someone, we give him or her a special name. She decided to call her dragon Riki.

For several days, staring at the stars, she longed for Riki. Until one day, a magical occurrence took place. The longing in her heart was so strong, she suddenly felt a force pull her inside the telescope.

For when you engage the universe, it will engage you back.

Her deep love for the dragon awakened the forces within, honoring the cosmic laws.

As Tea travelled through a force of bright light at breathtaking speed, she braced herself for a landing in an unknown land. When she opened her eyes, she found herself floating in space… her father's study no longer there; instead 200 billion stars surrounded her.

"Maybe Riki is traveling to…" and before she could complete her thought, WHOOOSHH!!! whispered a solar wind, as it lifted her onto the planet known as The Kingdom of the Fuzzy Wuzzies.

The Kingdom of the Fuzzy Wuzzies was a beautiful place to begin a search for such a mysterious being,for it was the tiniest planet in the whole cosmos — a beautiful space full of roses with

stems so long they seemed to stare at the sky, and dance in the cosmic wind blowing through galaxies.

If you took the time to pause, then you too would see that these flowers, indeed, perfumed the moment.

"Mmmm, Chocolate smelling roses!"

Suddenly, she heard the pitter-patter of feet behind her and the quaintest little voice that sounded like it came from a very tiny creature.

"Quick... over here!" said the voice.

Tea looked and saw nothing.

"Psst... I am right here!" the voice ushered, *"under the rose."*

Tea looked down and saw a tiny creature shaped like a fuzzy ball. It was bright yellow in color with purple eyes that stood out like grapes. The creature looked cross-eyed and agitated, as it motioned her to bend down. Tea got down on her hands and knees bewildered by the creature.

She approached the creature to have a closer look, but the creature wouldn't have any of it.

"Quick!" it said rather rudely, *"follow me!"*

And just like that, the two began a mad chase through a mad haze of a complex labyrinth of shrubs and chocolate smelling roses. Round and round and round they ran, as the creature led Tea along the path of the labyrinth.

"We are running," said the creature.

"We are running, why is that?" asked Tea, trying to catch her breath, which one could no longer distinguish from the smell of chocolate smelling roses.

The creature glanced at her in panic, but didn't answer. Together they ran, as though playing a game of cat and mouse, gasping for air but never stopping.

"Where are we running to?"

"Are you not afraid?" the creature asserted with great urgency.

"Afraid of what?" asked the little girl.

"You are not from here!" the creature quickly surmised, his purple grape eyes more crossed than ever.

"Oh..."

The creature's eyes widened with curiosity and disapproval, all the same it continued down the labyrinth.

The Fuzzy Wuzzy wanted to know why the little girl was not afraid, but was afraid to ask her.

For in life, we have a choice to accept the unknown or deny it. The cosmic law says:

All those who embrace the unknown, will discover a key to a new universe.

"I am taking you to the edge."

"You are taking me to the...?"

The creature with the crossed grape eyes, who had never looked a little girl in the eye before, made a great rumbling sound, then said, *"you are NOT a Fuzzy Wuzzy!!!"*

Before Tea could process her first encounter with a Fuzzy Wuzzy, or notice that it was yellow and fuzzy and she was not, they came upon the edge of the planet. Tea had just enough time to read the creature's badge: INSPECTOR BORDER CONTROL, before the creature crossed his grape eyes one last time, and pushed her off the planet of the Fuzzy Wuzzies.

THE ORACLE

The little girl fell off the planet of the Fuzzy Wuzzies hard and fast, escaping the weak gravitational waves that appeared like ripples in space. She landed on a dwarf planet in a haze of cosmic dust that carried the information of stars. The dwarf planet was far different from the Planet of the Fuzzy Wuzzies. It was rocky and full of potholes caused by falling meteorites that had once landed on the planet.

Tea stood still as a group of creatures observed her, rabbits and squirrels, frogs and gophers. They all stared at her, all but for an iridescent blue peacock who was curious just the same. He watched Tea from the corner of his eye, pretending that he didn't really notice her. For the peacock suffered from an excessive sense of self-importance. He, like Narcissus, had once looked in a pool of water and had fallen in love with his own image.

Finally! A fidgety frog, dressed in a purple suit and striped pants, stepped forward. He had his hair combed back and wore a boutonniere in the left breast pocket of his stylish striped purple suit, which he fiddled with out of habit every time he spoke.

"How may we address you? Madam, My lady, Ma Donna…?"

"Oh!" she responded, *"Please, help me. I am Tea! I am searching for a bird with magnificent wings."*

"Tarocchi!" Someone yelled.

"Yea… Tarocchi… Tarocchi!"

"Take her to Tarocchi," chimed another.

The frog agreed; fidgeting with his boutonniere, he bid the girl, *"follow me..."*

Tarocchi was a great oracle that lived on the other side of the Black Hole. A discussion about the girl's visit had taken place light years before. It was forewarned at the grand convention of oracles that a little girl seen travelling through the cosmos, would show up at the doorstep of an oracle looking for an elusive bird. The whole world would one day know her name as a result of the lessons she had learned in the cosmos.

Tarocchi moved to and fro nervously in his cave in anticipation. For how do you guide someone who does not know what he or she is searching for?

Tea and the fidgety frog, arrived upon the great oracle's cave that shone with a light so bright it illuminated the entire sky forcing Tea to cover her eyes. The frog bowed, and then motioned with both arms, bidding her to do the same.

A small creak sounded and the wise oracle walked out from the cave.

"A deck of cards!" said Tea.

The fidgety frog, who had never introduced himself, presented Tea to Tarocchi.

"You are a deck of cards!" said Tea.

"Not just any deck of cards," cautioned the oracle. *"Each card has the wisdom to provide you with courage to make big changes along your journey...even changes within a little girl."*

"I am looking for a magnificent bird," Tea said, throwing her arms in the air to describe the dragon's wings.

"*Ah,*" said Tarocchi, "*you mean to say the bird who flew so high he transformed himself into a dot in the sky, no longer visible to the human eye?*"

"*Yes!*"

"*All I can do is act as a pointer and point you in a direction,like a moon on a dark night, like an arrow or a sign on a dead end road, nothing more, nothing less. You alone determine the way by the choices you make.*"

The frog was privy to a reunion between a young hero and a guardian in space. For a hero is someone who lets go of everything ordinary he or she knows, in search of a higher truth. A hero creates a new path, travels on it and then gifts this path to others.

"*Close your eyes,*" Tarocchi said to Tea.

And she did.

"*Tell me, what do you see?*"

"*I see stars,*" said Tea.

"*O.K., now take away the stars. Try to be empty,empty like a vessel with no water,empty like a night with no stars. Now what do you see?*"

"*I…I see nothing... I hear a voice.*"

The oracle's face lit up.

The little girl shut her eyes, listening to the sound of her inner voice, for it sang a beautiful melody in her heart.

"*Now, step forward and draw a card.*"

Tea stepped forward and drew a card from within the oracle.

"My, oh my!" Tarocchi gasped. *"No one has drawn this card in a long, looooooong time."*

"Which card did I draw?"

"You have drawn the Princess of Veary Vee
The card of secret magic and
potential mystery.
You must .nd the magic of Veary Vee,
where birds and dragons .y free! Free! Free!"

Tea's eyes widened- *"did you say birds?"*

"This card indicates you are going to be learning some very odd things. Very odd!"

Tea trusted the guardian out in space.

"The universe is a weird place to be, weird things happen here!"

Like all mentors, the oracle does not show you the truth itself. He did not tell Tea who was the great magical creature she had seen. It was her journey to discover.

The little girl thought of the danger ahead of her quest.

"This is your adventure. Not mine..." said the oracle.

Saying this, he pointed Tea in a direction toward the night.

Tea left the oracle and followed the dark and empty night. Her eyes shone like embers, guided by her inner light.

As she floated through space, she saw the universe unveil before her eyes. She noticed how the space around each floating object appeared so still, yet a disorder of comets and meteors constantly whizzed by her. She thought of her heart and the space within her heart and wondered if a charming prince would ever find his way inside.

She thought of the yellow fuzzy creature she had met, and the borders she had crossed. It reminded her so much of the lines and borders that separate people on a map, how intangible lines are easily crossed.

Finally, she thought of the voice inside and wondered what it would say to her if she listened.

ILLUSIONS

"Hi, Tea!" said a voice.

Tea felt a hand grasp hers. It was a creature just like her; only it was white as snow and had eyes blue as the deepest part of the ocean. The creature looked like it carried the sea in its eyes.

Tea smiled at it. For though, they had never met, she had an overwhelming feeling she had known this creature her entire life.

"How do you know me?" Tea questioned.

The snow-skinned creature with the sea in its eyes did not answer.

"Are you happy to see me?" said the creature.

Far more important than knowing someone's name, age or job, was how we felt in their presence.

Indeed, Tea was happy.

Together, creature and girl floated hand-in-hand, until they reached a land that looked like an empty blue desert. The light from a giant moon illuminated the universe; it made the surface of the sea glisten like pearls.

Tea chased the elusive snow-skin creature, playing with it, until a voice behind called out...

"And, just where do you think you're going?"

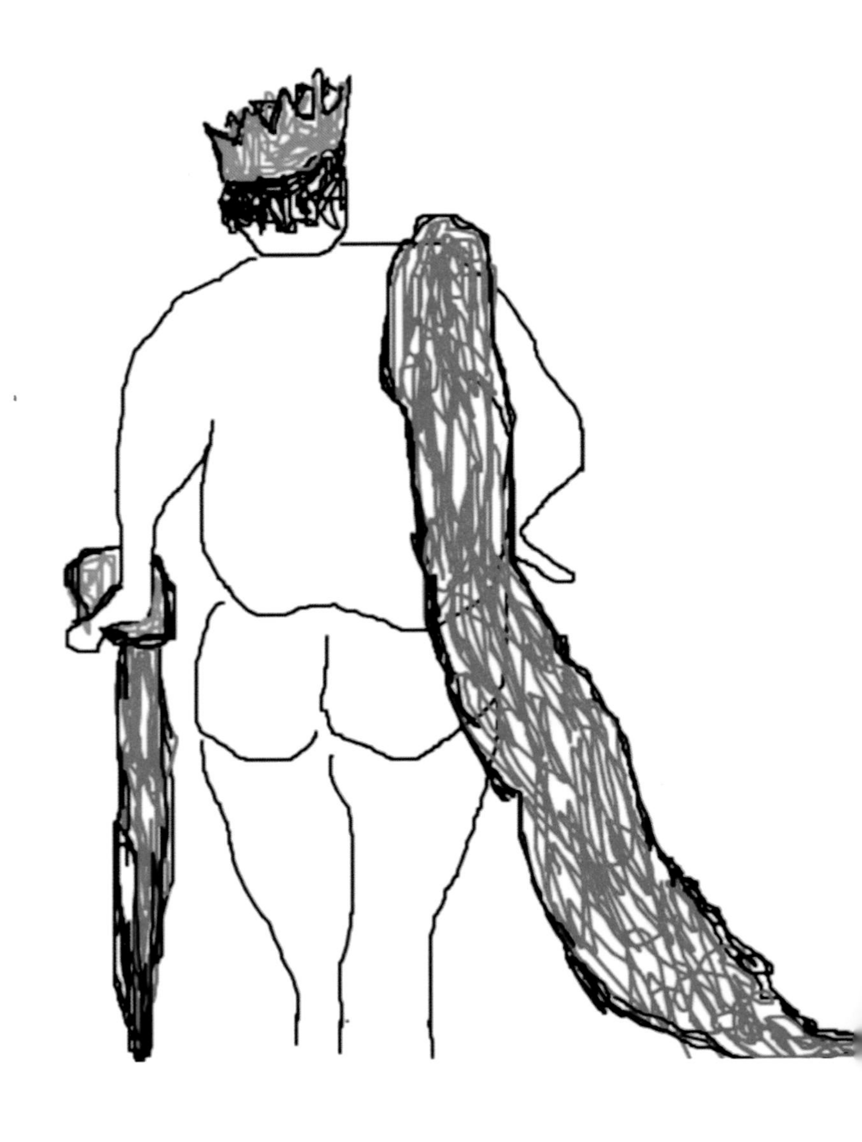

Startled, Tea and the snow-skin creature looked back and saw a peculiar looking man, stark naked, with a crown on his head, a red velvet cape on his right shoulder, and a gold scepter in his hand.

"Don't just stand there," he blurted, *"say something!"*

Tea looked on in disbelief. Meanwhile, the creature responded, *"You look marvelous, Your Highness! And the colors! Oh, the colors on your fabric are striking. I have never seen anything like it!"*

And the vain, naked king looked on with approval.

"Oh!" gasped Tea, *"I know you... you're the emperor from the fairy tale* 'The Emperor's New Clothes'!" [This is a beloved fairy tale by Hans Christian Andersen.]

And the Emperor, realizing he had been caught, didn't want to admit he lived in fairy tales, so he HUFFED and PUFFED and shuffled past Tea and her new friend, pretending he had somewhere to go.

"Oh..."

"Watch, just a few more steps and we will come to my castle," said the snow-skinned creature with the sea in its eyes.

"You live in a castle?" interrupted Tea, "you must be a princess!"

"I am a princess!"

Walking at a fast pace, the snow-white beast moved forward as the little girl followed. Suddenly, the creature stopped, mid-step.

"This is my castle," the creature exclaimed, pointing at the empty space.

"This is your castle...but there's nothing here!" said Tea, spinning around the empty space.

"It is an imaginary castle and I am an imaginary princess!" said the creature.

Tea felt uneasy talking to what appeared to be an illusion.

"Why did you tell me you are a princess?"

"Because you wanted to meet a princess, just like you wanted to meet the naked emperor!" said the creature, its eyes opening wide, allowing Tea to see the ebb and flow of the ocean.

Tea wondered who this creature really was.

"Where do you live?" Tea exclaimed, her brow furrowing, as she earnestly tried to discern reality from unreality.

The snow-skinned creature shrugged its shoulders. *"I don't really know. You imagined me, you imagined the vain emperor, and you imagined all of this. If you are thirsty, all you have to do is imagine a well and drink from it."*

As Tea began to think about the strange words coming out of the creature, it suddenly vanished. And so did the planet, and so did the blue desert, and so did the emperor.

A SCORPION NAMED STING

Tea found herself once again floating in space. In the distance, she spotted a comet. As the comet zoomed by Tea grabbed its tail, but she let go almost immediately as one would if one inadvertently held a hot cup of tea.

Falling backwards, she landed on an island surrounded by vast ocean.

"Ouch!" said a scorpion as he looked at her.

Tea looked around and saw that the island was so small there was just enough room for a little girl and a scorpion.

"How do you do?" Tea curtsied politely, with one hand held out and the other rubbing her bruised bottom.

"You fell so mighty and quick, I thought you were a shooting star," chuckled the scorpion.

"I have fallen many times," said Tea.

"That is wonderful, wonderful!" chuckled the scorpion.

"What is so wonderful about falling?" asked Tea.

"Well, the rising!" said the scorpion with a smile. *"Every fall has a rising! It's the same stuff that makes a sun rise so beautifully every morning or a little girl stand tall."*

Tea had never thought of rising and falling. She remembered the words of the oracle -you *will learn some very odd things... very odd.*

"Are you a poet?"

"I am a shrink," said the proud scorpion, indignantly.

"A shrimp?"

"No! A shrink," said the scorpion, who had been mistaken for a shrimp before, *"I solve problems."*

Saying those words, he rattled the end of his segmented tail.

"Oh," replied Tea, who had never spoken to a shrink before.

"Do you have a problem?" asked the scorpion, a keen smile now drawing itself slowly across his face.

"Yes!"

"Wonderful, wonderful!" chuckled the scorpion.

"Do you have a big problem?"

"Yes, it has wings to fly!"

The scorpion suddenly realized, that this was the very girl with a magical destiny the creatures had been forewarned would come wandering into the cosmos in search of the Great Dragon!

"Oh I seeee..." said the scorpion, mischievously, trying to hide his awe for the phenomena that was about to unfold. His eyes went back and forth from one corner to the other, his segmented tail flopped from one side to the other rhythmically — he never thought the prophesied girl would fall right into his hands!

The scorpion turned his back to ponder how he could take advantage.

"*Shrink*," she said, making the scorpion turn and face her, "*What about my problem?*"

"*What about it?*"

"*You haven't asked me about the bird.*"

"*Why in heavens would I do such a thing?*"

"*What do you mean by that?*"

The scorpion discounted her.

"*Well, how will I find him?*"

"*Why, with a rainbow, darling, a sunrise, and sometimes even a handful of chocolates!*" said the scorpion.

"*With a rainbow, a sunrise and a handful of chocolates???*"

"*Forget the bird*," said the scorpion furiously, "*look around you...*"

When Tea looked around she saw that the ocean, now no longer blue, glistened like melted gold, for the sun was rising and its sparkling reflection filled the entire expanse of the inbound tide. And while the rest of the world lay nestled in bed, eyes closed and dreaming, the little girl witnessed her first mystical sunrise…and her spirit shined bright and golden as the sun itself.

The scorpion chuckled. "*You want to talk about your mystical experience with the bird, but it is of no interest to me. I have important business clients waiting on the other side of this shore. Just remember, when you want to count your problems, find a shore and count sunrises instead. Go each day and find a sunrise to look at. You will then become privy to the magic of the cosmos.*"

As the scorpion said this, Tea saw the scorpion's narrow, segmented tail curve, and a glimpse of a sharp, silver pointed stinger suddenly appear within view.

The venom in the stinger could capture a prey, rendering it incapable of movement.

Tea's eyes grew wide; her tears hit the ground like the beads of a pearl necklace come undone.

But the scorpion stopped and slowly drew his dagger back in, his eyes moving to and fro, nervously.

"You were going to kill me?"

"For a moment… perhaps, but your innocence, disarmed me."

Unlike the Fuzzy Wuzzy, who pushed Tea off the planet because it did not know if she was bad or if she was good, the scorpion was used to killing creatures and thus welcoming its prey.

The scorpion had learned a valuable lesson:

Poison is far more lethal to the heart of the one who is giving it.

"I hurt you...," said the scorpion.

Tea turned to the scorpion, feeling especially sorry for the creature.

"You are not like anyone I have met before...," continued the scorpion, who realized he had made a big mistake.

Only kindness toward a devil creature makes a good heart. As much as Tea needed to view a sunrise, the scorpion needed to view several more…

The scorpion looked at the little girl, alarmed at the deep magic inside her. It tried to apologize but it was too late, for the little girl had seen that the scorpion had no love in his heart.

Tea went inside herself. Within, she saw the image of a seed and planted it inside the scorpion's heart. Like a seed dropped into the dirtiest soil, it too would take root and grow. In good time, perhaps it would blossom.

In suffering, it is always the injured who have the power to save.

"I have planted a seed in your heart," she said.

For to hurt, was always a solo act inflicted on oneself. This truth was gifted to Tea and to anyone who passes this story on...

Where one finds the greatest reason not to give to another, one should give for that reason.

"There is something magical about you..."

A huge downpour of rain suddenly fell from the sky.

As there seemed no escape from the island, two dolphins unexpectedly appeared in the horizon sent by a friend, Tea would soon encounter.

Tea left the scorpion without saying goodbye. For the love placed in the heart of an enemy was an infinite experience, no words could describe.

As Tea sat on one of the dolphin's back, the scorpion felt a sharp pain in his chest.

"I love you..." said the scorpion.

Just then a fern sprouted in the scorpion's heart.

....

The dolphins brought her to a shore and Tea thanked them and ran as fast as she could. Ahead, she saw a bright green neon sign that glittered in the distance. Inscribed on it were the words, DISH WAY.

Speaking to herself, she whispered, "*Which way is Dish Way?*

And the sign enchantingly responded, "*Whish way do you want to go?*"

"*Oh!*" Tea exclaimed, bringing her hands up to her cheeks, tickled that the sign, indeed, had a lisp. "*Pardon me, but I am searching for a bird who flew into the cosmos...*"

The sign knew instantly who she was looking for. For it too, had been foretold of a young girl, who would leave the ordinary world and come wandering through the cosmos in search of an elusive bird. The sign respected the universe's truth in all matters:

All guidance comes from within.

"*What doesh the bird look like, so I can point you to one?*" asked the sign.

"*It is magnificently large,*" she said with seriousness, throwing both her hands up in the air dramatically, "*almost the size of a mountain, with unearthly eyes and huge, fierce wings.*"

The entire cosmos knew of the Great Dragon. He was the most powerful creature in the cosmos.

"I haven't sheen any birdsh in light yearsh, but does a dog interest you?" asked the cosmic pointer.

"A dog? Out in space...," asked Tea, who was very familiar with dogs. " *Which way did the dog go?"*

And the sign spun around at lightning speed, before abruptly coming to a stop.

The sign read, "DISH WAY."

And following DISH WAY, Tea saw in the far distance a glimpse of a vibrant city, taken over by crawling plants and creepers that wrapped buildings.

While the message on the sign remained the same, her path had suddenly changed.

THE BUTTERFLY AND THE LION

"Oh, my!"

It was a cosmic jungle city overrun by trees taller than the buildings on Earth, and creatures so titillating and small, you had to squint to see them.

A baboon yelling in a high-pitch, alerted the animals to the presence of Tea, and they all scrambled, vanishing to watch her carefully from behind the trees. All, save one—a Great Shepherd dog that stood in the middle of the jungle with nobility.

"Did the dolphins find you?" the Noble Shepherd asked.

"It was you that sent for them?"

"Yes."

"How did you know…?"

"Are you the girl who has come to the cosmos to search for a bird?"

"Yes, that's me."

"I can help you," said the Noble Shepherd, *"my name is Archon."*

Archon was an enigma in the cosmos. His name symbolized a ruler or 'Grand Prince' who stood between the human race and God. He represented the voice of the animal kingdom.

Tea showed her appreciation, when Archon continued...

"The other animals may not accept you."

She remembered the Fuzzy Wuzzy creature.

"Humans have lost value for the heart. Each one of these animals has been hurt by a human."

Tea thought of the scorpion who solved the creatures' problems by killing them, neglecting his own heart.

"I have a heart that speaks to me..."

Her heart had grown from obedience to the lessons practiced in the cosmos. She looked deep into Archon's eyes, exposing her being like the spirit of a sunrise. As the animals looked into her eyes, they too saw a hint of all the hidden gardens they had played in.

They slowly came out from their hiding places exposed to the girl's good spirit. They too, had a mysterious animal spirit but it was the Great Noble Shepherd whose purpose stood out in her mind.

"Archon," she asked, *"where are you from?"*

"I am from PLANET NOT MUCH BIGGER THAN KANSAS. *My planet was destroyed. No child, animal or tree exists on my planet."*

"How does one do that?"

"Do what?"

"Destroy such a beautiful place?"

"Few people remember to look and see that we live in a beautiful, wonderful universe..."

The compulsive, obsessive way in which humans shop, use their cell phones, Internet and bank accounts is what Archon was referring to. They go to war with each other to bring peace.

Many have eyes. Not many have the eyes to see. Tea thought to herself.

"What are you searching for?"

"I am searching for the generosity of a little seed," said Archon.

The little girl took comfort that the Great Shepherd was also looking.

"What can a seed do?"

"In every seed, there is deeper magic," he said.

In every seed lies the dream of a hundred flowers, the breath of a thousand trees...

This was true. Even the grandest building on earth looked empty without a tree next to it.

"We are afraid of human technology!!" said the animals as they campaigned and made loud, banging noises like a protest rally.

"Even that big mammoth over there is scared of a girl like you," said a raccoon, pointing its sharp tapered finger at Tea's frame.

Tea paused to imagine the fear inside the heart of a big mammoth.

"People have great outer technology; but inner technology is lacking. You humans send rockets to the moon, command the tallest metals to rise up in the sky, yet your space engineers curl up under their blankets at night with sad hearts that cry," said a moth, "afraid to follow their heart."

This was true. On Earth, most people work compulsively, eat compulsively, and take medicine compulsively.

"You have weak hearts, this makes you an easy prey," shrilled a laughing hyena.

This was true. On the most desirable place on Earth: the value for money was far greater than the value for the heart. Heart attacks were the leading cause of death in leading cities.

"You need to develop your inner technology to discover your heart," said a wise owl.

"Inner technology. What is that?"

"It is the magic inside," Archon responded, *"it is as powerful as the sun."*

"If that ugly caterpillar can change into a butterfly, think how much you can transform. That is deeper magic!" said a sloth.

"Transform. What is that?" Tea asked turning her head upside down at the goby blue green caterpillar, whose universe was upside down.

"What? What? What?" asked the goby caterpillar, who found the conversation a bit weird.

"How do you become a butterfly?"

"I simply find the tip of a leaf of course, sit still… and wait for magical things to happen."

Human effort is the weakest force in the universe. Th is was certain.

"Don't be afraid to follow your heart, just because you are alone and troubled," said a lone wolf who had been a leader his entire life, *"a guide will show up inside."*

And Tea saw the magic of a leader that follows his heart. For the animals seemed to be telling her that far more potent than the "outer power" humans struggle to have, was a mysterious power inside.

It is a quiet place within, at the center of your being, that the deepest magic is discovered.

A seed becomes a redwood; a tadpole a human child, a caterpillar a butterfly — effortlessly. No outside technology could match the force. This was certain.

"Are you hungry?" asked Archon, who had taken a liking to Tea because she reminded him of a little girl he had played with on the PLANET NOT MUCH BIGGER THAN KANSAS.

"Indeed, I could eat anything!"

The animals then led her to a stone table, and there she had the best meal she had ever eaten and laughed with her new friends, who had so many weird things to say.

"My friends would never believe that I shared a meal with mammoths and Bengal tigers, lions and caterpillars."

They spent hours talking, laughing and listening to Tea's adventures of the Kingdom of the Fuzzy Wuzzies, as Tea remembered Tarocchi's words.

"Do you know where I can find the Princess of Veary Vee? She knows who I am searching for."

"Sure! Sure!" said an antelope, *"she lives by Third Star."*

"Uh-um. Tell me, how do you discover a dragon when you go through the entire cosmos looking for a bird?" asked a monkey, mocking the prophecy and fate of the little girl.

Archon, the Great Shepherd, calmly told the animals,

"Let each one find the magical journey to his heart."

As she said goodbye to her new friends, the caterpillar joyfully said, *"In a few hours, by the time you get home, I will become a butterfly!"*

Tea now knew that it is the Force that makes a beautiful butterfly.

As she left the animals, Archon came to her side. Looking especially sad, he said, *"You remind me of a girl I used to play with."*

The Great Shepherd and girl shared a moment of silence.

"What happened to her?"

"What happens to all of them? They forget to play, to count a sunrise, to follow their heart."

So many people on our planet are afraid, dear reader. The illusions that money, power and wealth will bring them capture them. True power is the ability to let go of what does not serve our hearts, to smile in the moment, and to explore what makes us happy more than the things that make us sad.

Children often have this power.

"Why don't you come and explore my heart?" Tea countered with the magic inherent in all children's hearts.

Archon accepted the invitation into her heart.

And just like that the two left the creatures unifying their journey.

They walked to the edge of the forest—where they found an isolated boxing ring on a platform. The red ropes of the ring were connected together between the posts. Sitting in the middle of the boxing ring was a pompous lion out in space.

"It's the King of the jungle!" Tea exclaimed.

She had never seen a lion outside of a cage.

As they approached the lion he jumped and pounced ferociously in the ring, and while his roar terrified Tea, curiosity got the better of her.

The lion looked at his audience approach and then let out a roar, *"I am preparing myself, and I am not quite king yet!"*

"Preparing for what?"

"A deadly opponent. He is the only one I have not beaten. If left unbeaten, I will never be king," said the lion, never stopping his successive flips and dips.

He growled and flexed his paws, wrestling the empty space.

"I prepare for my fight each day, by waking up early in the morning, running by the ocean and witnessing a sunrise..." the proud lion off ered.

Tea, did not care to know why people who work in an office had high blood pressure, cancer, obesity, and stress...

Or about the lives of the people who died prematurely of heart attacks...

She was interested in how a warrior enjoyed perfect health, sound body, mind and spirit.

"But aren't you afraid to hurt your face?" she asked, *"isn't the ring violent?"*

"Kids play fight; tiger cubs play fight. Fighting is not inherently bad, just the opposite. Marriage, on the other hand, that's rough."

And the lion continued...

"The ring you speak of is the stillest place to be. It has allowed me to see 20 sunrises this month..."

For, the lion trained his spirit more than his body. To do this he looked for the celestial sun. As the light of the sun upholds the entire universe, the light of the lion's spirit maintained his body.

To win any battle, more than violence, one needed peace. *And, the light of the celestial sun provided that.*

Tea saw the heart of a warrior was different than that of an ordinary human being. He lets go of the comfort of daily routine in search of a deeper meaning to life. To do this, he wakes up with a sunrise, runs to the top of a mountain, runs through a forest, past vibrant colors, flowers and trees and he feels at peace. All this he does to discover a quiet place within, the essence of his being.

For, the journey of a hero was no different than that of a seed.

It was similar to the journey a seed makes to discover its essence. It is an unknown path full of obstacles for a seed dropped in the dirtiest soil to become a flower. Yet, the seed fights with all its might, in order to perfume the moment.

But who was the lion training to battle?

"He must be a formidable foe to take on a dominant lion as you!"

"He is," roared the lion in a terrifying voice. *"He is faster than a cheetah and hits harder than a herd of elephants. He hits without hitting and moves without moving. He uses no technique. My technique is his technique."*

Tea was on an impatient mission.

"I cannot stay..."

As Tea curtsied goodbye, to the lion that so desperately wanted to be king, the sun gradually set once again — its cycle complete.

"He is here!" the lion fiercely said.

No one showed up. Tea looked down at the lion's paw. Lying under his feet was his shadow.

Tea was astonished by this unfamiliar truth.

"What a strange lion he is; his greatest enemy is himself."

But a hero's journey is not to fear the path, but to embrace it the more unfamiliar it becomes...

The Great Shepherd came to Tea's side and they tracked the Princess of Veary Vee in the direction of Th ird Star.

Meanwhile, history would one day show that the battle against self is never ending...

MADMAN

For days Tea and Archon walked through the forest. Day-after-day, the planet's forest never seemed to end until one morning they saw a bright beam of light filtering its way through the leaves. Tea ran towards it, hoping to find the Princess of Veary Vee behind the foliage. Instead, what the foliage revealed was a man in a golden cage.

Archon jumped in front of Tea, for it was his nature to sacrifice for others.

"Should we be afraid?" Tea asked, walking up to the golden cage.

"Afraid of me?" the man jested, pointing at himself.

The man in the golden cage laughed so loud that both Archon and Tea joined in.

"Laughter is contagious!" he said. *"Doctors tell me I have a contagious laugh."* And, once again, he broke out in a peal of maddening laughter that could be heard throughout space and time.

"Why are you in a golden cage?" Tea asked.

"Who is in a cage?" he asked curiously.

The handsomely dressed madman, once again, broke into maddening laughter. Tea and Archon, found themselves laughing every time he laughed.

"Why, this is a cage of my own making." Saying that, he grinned, pulled out a golden key.

"But who are you, really?"

"I thought it was obvious! I am a Madman! Or the Man with the Golden Key, or simply the Man in a Golden Cage."

"A Madman?"

"Perhaps."

The Madman seemed very pleased about insanity.

"Why, what makes you so mad?"

"It depends on who has who locked in a cage."

"What do you mean?"

"I want to be free, not just from this cage of course... from a system, from a book, from other realities dictated to me. I want to be free from my self."

The little girl thought of freedom from society, which the mad man spoke of. All great thinkers were once deemed mad! Once misunderstood! Some were guillotined, others burned at the stake, and the ones who survived were caged.

"Can you free yourself from the cage?"

The Madman promptly produced the golden key and unlocked himself.

"Now who is in the cage?"

"Certainly, I am not," said Tea.

"Lets hope," said the Madman as he grimaced, twitching his jaw nervously.

Saying that, he tickled Tea. He was a very unpredictable character.

"What do you know about this path?" asked Madman.

Tea thought of the teachings.

"I am on a journey to discover what is in my heart..."

The little girl felt deep despair thinking of the dragon.

"Well, when you find a boy," continued the Madman, *"make sure he gives you his heart...not a cage."*

"Why would anyone offer a cage?" asked Tea.

And the Madman broke into a loud shrilling and spine-curling laugh!

"Happiness is a land unknown to human beings." This time the Madman did not laugh.

"When you hug someone who hurts you enough times, it becomes a posture in life... happiness is the light you shine from inside," **said Archon, the Great Shepherd.**

He was teaching the girl about the ultimate sacrifice.

Once again, the Madman broke out into laughter so loud it shook the entire star.

"Have you found the place of happiness?" said Tea.

The Madman took a few steps inside the golden cage and said:

"When I free my heart…I will know that place."

Tea remembered her quest.

"Do you know where the Princess of Veary Vee lives?"

"If you float on a cloud, it will bring you to Veary Vee," said the Madman matter-of-factly.

"How can we be so sure?" asked Tea, softy. *"I have lost my way so many times."*

"You may lose yours, but clouds never lose their way," said the Madman referring to the way. This time he did not laugh.

Archon thanked him. Turning around, they walked forward a few steps when Tea quickly turned her back and yelled, *"Mr. Madman…"*

"Yeeeeees…?"

"You never told me why you lock yourself in a golden cage?"

"And, you never told me why you trap your feelings for a certain little boy, inside."

Saying this, he put out a huge laugh into the galaxy.

Tea thought about the Madman's words. There was a little boy she had feelings for far, far away. Feelings she had learned to trap inside.

Tea and Archon boarded a cloud and let it take them where all clouds went.

As they floated away, the Madman yelled, *"Your teeth are smiling, but is your heart?"* Saying that, he burst out into his loudest laughter yet.

And Tea realized what this meant.

In life, every day routine was simply— fear, learned responses and limits that bore boring results! ***A fairy tale could only blossom in one who has the courage to follow his or her heart. This was certain.***

MIDDLE OF NOWHERE

As the great mysterious Archon and Tea continued their journey, the cloud stopped by an abandoned brown house, a sort of celestial travel stop.

Tea walked up to the door and found it open. Inside, it was pitch dark.

"Hello?" Tea called out into the darkness, singing the last "o's" of her hello.

"Hello," echoed the voice.

"Who are you?" questioned Tea.

"Who are you?" responded the voice in kind.

"Oh!" exclaimed Tea. *"It's so dark in here, I can't see a thing."*

Right then, Tea heard a click and a big mushroom-shaped lamp illuminated the entire room.

The light showed a colorful room full of artifacts from all over the world. Each wall was covered with eclectic little knick-knacks - exquisite, bright orange plates from Mexico, hieroglyph papyri from Egypt, a samurai sword from Japan, and rare green jade from China.

In the middle of the room an old man with a white beard sat on the couch. He wore purple, star-shaped glasses that glittered like jazzy stars.

"Howdy!" he said.

"Are you a decorator?" asked Tea, who always questioned everything.

"Nope," said the strange looking man.

Beside him was a bookshelf with encyclopedias of every kind you could imagine. Tea picked up a large book that lay open called THE MIDDLE OF NOWHERE and flipped through the pages.

"That's a good one," said the man with the white beard. *"I've tried to get there my whole life."*

"THE MIDDLE OF NOWHERE? It really exists?" asked a wide-eyed Tea.

"It is said that a princess was once spotted, hunched over a fishing rod on the edge of a planet in the middle of nowhere."

"A princess with a fishing rod?" exclaimed Tea with wonder. *"What was she fishing for?"* she continued.

"For a wish!"

"How do you fish for a wish?"

"You cast your invisible string into the universe, and wait for magical and heavenly things to happen."

The little girl's eyes grew wide as she thought of the caterpillar.

To move a mountain, one needs to be still.

"Sometimes your eff orts," continued the old man, *"get in your way."*

"You must believe in your power. Your mind can be a wishing tree. Anything you want can happen and bear fruit."

"My mind is a wishing tree…," the little girl said to herself.

"The power inside you is the greatest force in the universe," said the old man.

"More magic?"

"Do you know you have the power to make this entire universe disappear?"

"What do you mean?"

"Close your eyes..."

And she did and everything disappeared.

"Deeper magic…" the old man said with a wink, *"play with it."*

"But, where is NOWHERE?" asked the little girl pointing at the book.

"It's a trick of words. NOWHERE is really NOW and HERE. It's the most difficult place for the mind to be."

"It is a riddle!" exclaimed Tea, *"I love riddles!"*

"Well, then," chuckled the old man with star-shaped jazzy glasses. *"When you get to my age, you will have solved several riddles of life."*

Tea moved about the space, distracted.

"To visit nowhere, one must learn to be still."

"Are you an explorer?" Tea questioned, as she flipped through the many exquisite landscapes in the book.

"Indeed, I have explored many places." And the old man shut his eyes for a long time.

Tea heard a few taps on the window and realized that Archon was giving her an indication.

"Sir, I should love to sit and hear your stories about your journey to NOW and HERE, but I must, in fact, find the Princess of Veary Vee."

And as Tea said that, the old man sighed, and said nothing.

He got up and started walking toward the door. As he moved forward, he stretched his hands out in front of him, making small motions, caressing the gravitational forces. He walked past the end of the sofa, and the edge of a coff ee table, before reaching the door.

When Tea got to where the old man stood, he pulled open her hand and squeezed into it a handful of chocolates.

"For your troubles...," he said.

The little girl suddenly remembered the scorpion's words about the magic contained in a handful of chocolates. She stared deep into the old man's eyes, trying to decipher his nature.

"Th ank you," said Tea, surprised to discover that the old man was blind. Yet, he was able to see the deepest part of her.

"Many places will capture your eyes, but only one will capture your heart..."

Tea stood still. And for the second time on her journey she wept, for the voice of a heart unheard makes a frail sound.

Saying that, the old man pulled on the cord of the mushroom shaped lamp and, once again, the room was pitch-black.

Tea left, realizing that her heart had stopped as she suddenly let her feelings for a certain little boy permeate the entire universe.

THE MAGIC OF VEARY VEE

Tea, Archon, and the cloud continued their journey. Floating on a cloud was like eating cotton candy. You never really felt like it was there.

Together they marveled at the universe, watching the bright lights against the dark solar system. They saw comets whiz by, leaving twinkling trail of cosmic dust. The thing about space was that if you blinked, you could miss the brilliance of a thousand stars. Tailless asteroids spun around Tea and life seemed like an orchestra of dazzling planets that shone like rainbows around the sun.

It had been exactly a while since Tea had last let out a yawn. For in space, time has no relevance.

"You need a place to rest," said Archon who was familiar with the charm contained in the yawn of a little girl.

"Archon," she interrupted, *"can anyone hear you?"*

"No."

"Why can't anyone hear your voice?"

"Because it takes courage to listen to one's heart."

Tea paused.

"All of the universe exists inside you. Even the voices you hear. Space is soundless."

The little girl looked at the universe around her and the stars reflected in her eyes. For the magic that surrounds us, few have the eyes to see.

No amount of money could replace the smell of a celestial rose,

or the vision of a sunrise...

the presence of a mountain,

or the spirit of a prince that takes a little girl by the hand.

Children, having so little, understood these things.

"Few grown-ups remember..." Archon said, *"that the magic of the universe comes at no price at all."*

They run after money, but the biggest price is paid with their heart.

Tea closed her eyes so she would remember.

As Archon finished his thought, the cloud brought them to the throne of the Princess of Veary Vee. There, the most beautiful enchantress Tea had ever seen stood by the Throne of Knowledge. It was just as Tarocchi had described. She wore a crescent moon on her head and a gown made of radiant pink diamonds. She stood tall and eff ervescent in front of a grand red curtain.

"How can I help you?" said the Enchantress, *"daughter, you have been blessed with a Great Destiny."*

Tea bowed, to the Enchantress.

"The oracle Tarocchi said you could help me find my bird who flew away."

The enchanting Princess paused. *"You mean to say,"* she continued, *"the dragon that flew so high, it transformed itself into a dot in the sky, no longer visible to the human eye?"*

The little girl was stunned.

"It was a Dragon?"

"Not just a dragon... The Great Dragon. The most powerful Dragon in the entire cosmos," said the Princess of Veary Vee, waving both her hands dramatically in the air.

Tea stood still.

"You came after the Dragon because, like him, you are looking to be free! Free! Free!" the Enchantress replied, offering her hands up to the sky.

"But, I am not in a cage!" said Tea, remembering the Man with the Golden Key.

"Some cages are invisible, invisible cages hide the most vicious creatures."

Tea thought of the cages on Earth that locked animals, mad men and criminals. People, however, roamed freely.

Maybe some humans are trapped in cages they cannot see.

As Tea made this realization, the wisdom in her mind blossomed.

"You need not worry," laughed the enchanting Princess, *"the Great Dragon has blessed you with a Great Destiny. You will be known throughout the corners of your world and ours."*

Archon, the Great Shepherd, nodded to further affirm the destiny of the girl was no different than that of a mountain flower.

"You will be the happiest girl on your planet because you follow obediently the teachings of the cosmos. You will share this cosmic message with your world. Now take seven steps forward. The magic of Veary Vee is behind that magnificent curtain," said the enchantress.

Tea, curious to discover the magic of Veary Vee, took seven steps forward. She anticipated the great secret about to be given to her and the change she would bring to the world.

Lifting the curtain, she blurted out, *"a hand mirror!"*

She grabbed the handle, looked at it, and a power of light forced its way like a tunnel out of the mirror.

Her exclamation caused even the Madman on Th ird Star to break into a maddening laugh that echoed and bounced throughout the entire universe.

When Tea glanced away, the mirror returned to ordinary. As soon as she glanced back, a force of intense light poured out.

"But, I thought I would find the Great Dragon."

"It is the Great Dragon who will find you," said the Princess of Veary Vee. *"This is the great secret kept for ages in the cosmos."*

It is our guide that finds us.

What did the Dragon tell you before he flew," prodded the Princess.

Tea immersed in mind, thought deeply...

"That he would come to me..."

And the enchanting Princess and Tea shared a moment of cosmic silence.

"This mirror is not as ordinary as it may look," cautioned the Princess of Veary Vee, *"and your search for a greater power is no different than your search for the Great Dragon. Look in the mirror..."*

When the Tea did this, a force of light poured out and propelled the handle to shake in her grasp.

"You are stronger than all the elements in the world...," she heard a voice say.

"Dragon!!!" she exclaimed.

The voice had come from within her.

Tea realized this was the same force contained in a little seed.

Tea thought of how long and how far her journey had taken her. For the first time, she realized what this journey was truly about.

"Listen to your heart..."

Saying that, the princess waved her wand around Tea and Archon, six times and, just like that, the little girl and the dog found themselves outside their home on planet Earth.

They began chasing each other in pure delight. For, while they said nothing, their hearts communicated the love they shared.

Tea and the dog were playing in the garden when Tea's mother came by.

"Where in the world have you been, Tea?" She asked.

Tea, remembering that grown-ups see only from the outside, decided to say nothing of the blueprint inside her heart.

Tea's mother grabbed the dog's leash.

"I thought I told you not to let Kansas play in mommy's rose garden!"

As Tea, exhausted by her journey, cheerfully followed her mother into the house for some delicious crepes, a butterfly flew by. As it did so, it laughed mysteriously.

"Look!" said Tea elatedly to Kansas, pointing at the butterfly.

Even further away, dear reader, on a planet far invisible to the human eye, there was a princess rushing hurriedly someplace with a fishing rod in one hand and a charming prince in the other! This was the same princess the old man had spoken of.

Both smiled, as two individuals often do when they share a secret.

So tonight, dear reader, when you close your eyes and the world ceases to exist, remember, that this is a weird, beautiful and wonderful universe where fairytales come true for those who will believe...

This was certain.

The End